The Three Little Pigs

ILLUSTRATED BY KATE DAVIES

Story adapted by
Christine Deverell

Once upon a time there were three little pigs, and one summer's day they decided to go out into the big, wide world on their own. As they walked along a forest path they talked about what they would do. "·We will each need to find a piece of land and build

ourselves a house to live in," said one little pig to his friends.

They passed a man with a cart piled high with straw.

The first little pig asked the man if he could have some straw

to build himself a house. The man was glad to give him

straw, and the little pig waved goodbye to the other two,

built a house and was very pleased with himself.

Soon, an old grey wolf came by, and when he saw the

straw house he stopped and looked through the window.

Inside he saw the little pig. So he went to the door, knocked

gently and said, in his sweetest voice, "Little pig, little pig,

can I come in?" And the little pig answered, "No, not by the

hair of my chinny, chin, chin." "Then I'll huff, and I'll puff,

and I'll blow your house down," growled the wolf. He huffed, and he puffed, and he blew the house down.

Meanwhile the other little pigs walked on, until they met a man carrying a cartload of twigs. One of the little pigs said to the man, "Would you give me some of these twigs to build a house?" And the man was glad to give him the twigs. The little pig waved goodbye to his friend, built a house and was very pleased with himself.

Soon, the old grey wolf came by, and when he saw the twig house he stopped and looked through the window. Inside he saw the second little pig. So he went to the door,

knocked gently and said, in his sweetest voice, "Little pig,
little pig, can I come in?" And the little pig answered, "No,
not by the hair of my chinny, chin, chin." "Then I'll huff, and

I'll puff, and I'll blow your house down," growled the wolf.

He huffed, and he puffed, and he blew the house down.

Now the third little pig was much smarter than the other two. He saw a man with a cartload of bricks, and he thought, "This is just what I need." So he begged the man to let him have enough bricks to build himself a house, and the man was happy to give him as many as he wanted. So the little

pig built himself a fine brick house with a kitchen and a big fireplace. Along came the wolf who knocked on the door and said, "Little pig, little pig, can I come in?" And the little pig answered, "No, not by the hair of my chinny, chin, chin." "Then I'll huff, and I'll puff, and I'll blow your house down," growled the wolf.

And he huffed, and he puffed, and he huffed, and he puffed, but no matter how hard he huffed and puffed, the wolf could not blow the house down. The little pig laughed at the wolf through the window. The wolf made a plan. "If I want to eat this pig," he said to himself, "then I will have to

trick him."

So he called, "Little pig, little pig, I know where there is a lovely field of turnips." "Where?" asked the little pig. "Behind farmer Smith's house; and if you are ready at six

o'clock tomorrow morning, I will call for you, and we can go together." "Very well. I will be ready," said the little pig. But the little pig got up at five o'clock, ran to farmer Smith's field, filled a sack with turnips and was safely back in his house when the wolf called for him at six. "Are you ready,

little pig?" called the wolf. "Ha, ha!" laughed the pig, "I thought you said to be ready at five. I have already been to the turnip field and now I am making a stew for my dinner."

The wolf was very angry, but in a sweet, gentle voice he said, "Little pig, there is a fine apple orchard at Oakwood Farm. Be ready at five tomorrow and we will go together." "Very well," said the little pig, "I'll see you tomorrow."

But the little pig got up at four and made his own way to the apple orchard. He climbed a tree to fill his sack, and just as he was about to come down, he saw the wolf approaching. The wolf called up to him, "Ah, little pig, you

did not wait for me. Are they nice apples?"

"Yes, absolutely delicious; I will throw one to you,"

said the pig. He threw it as far as he could, so that as the

wolf ran to catch it, the little pig jumped down

from the tree and ran home as fast as he could.

The next day the wolf

knocked at the little

pig's door and

said, "There is a

fair in the town this

afternoon, will you be going?" "Oh yes," said the little pig

excitedly, "I love going to the fair; what time will you be

ready?" "At three o'clock," said the wolf. As usual, the little

pig left home early and made his way to the fair alone. He

bought himself a butter churn, and was on his way home with it when he saw the wolf coming along the road towards him.

He quickly climbed into the butter churn, and set it rolling down the hill and heading straight for the wolf. The wolf was so frightened that he turned tail and ran all the way home again. Later that evening the

wolf went to the little pig's house. He stood

at the door telling his sad tale of how

frightened he had been at the sight of a

butter churn coming at him at great speed.

Then the little pig laughed at him

and said, "That was me inside the butter

churn!" This made the wolf very angry indeed, and he

growled, "I will eat you up, I will, I will.

I am going to come down the chimney to get you!" As the

wolf climbed up onto the roof the little pig stoked up the fire

in the huge fireplace, and put a pot of water on to boil.

The wolf fell down the chimney and landed in the pot. The wolf jumped out of the pot never to return again and the little pig lived safely and happily in his brick house for many years.